Copyright © 2025 by Artima & Marcus Thornton.

All rights reserved. No part of this book may be used or reproduced in any form whatsoever without written permission except in the case of brief quotations in critical articles or reviews.

Printed in the United States of America.

ISBN: 9798305203721

Imprint: Independently published

Chapter 1: Unearthing Shadows

The room was dim, bathed in the soft, amber glow of a single desk lamp. Shadows stretched and twisted across the walls as if reaching toward Tamika, mirroring the fear and tension building within her. She moved from corner to corner, her mind racing as she replayed everything she'd uncovered over the past few months.

On the coffee table lay a leather-bound notebook, worn and frayed at the edges, its pages filled with names, dates, and connections she had painstakingly pieced together. Each word was a revelation, a clue pointing to something larger and far more sinister than she had ever imagined. But now, the story was becoming disturbingly clear: beneath the surface of her quiet community, a dark force thrived, and it was powerful enough to keep everyone silent.

At the center of it all was a name whispered in hushed tones, never spoken aloud without a wary glance around: the Circle.

Tamika sat on the edge of the couch; her gaze fixed on the open notebook. Every entry held a fragment of the story, a shadow of something bigger, older, and terrifyingly organized. She hadn't meant to dig so deep. But the deeper she went, the more she realized just how much was hidden in plain sight. And now, as she stared at the ink that threatened to reveal her own fate, she understood that the Circle was more than a rumor—it was a silent, omnipresent force, lurking in the places no one thought to look.

The sound of a knock, soft and hesitant, broke her concentration, and her heart leaped to her throat. She knew that knock. She hadn't told Jamal the full extent of what she'd found, only that she needed to see him. She hadn't even wanted to bring him into this nightmare, but she couldn't face it alone anymore. She needed someone she could trust.

She took a steadying breath, feeling her hands tremble slightly as she reached for the door handle. After tonight, she knew there would be no turning back.

Jamal stepped inside, and his presence filled the small room with a quiet intensity. Tall and broad-shouldered, he was someone she had always thought of as a calming presence. But tonight, something in his demeanor was different. His expression was guarded, and his eyes flicked around the room, resting for a moment on the open notebook on her coffee table.

"You've been busy," he said finally, his voice low and measured. There was something in his tone—apprehension, maybe even fear—that he couldn't entirely hide.

"I needed answers," Tamika replied, her voice steadier than she felt. She moved to the couch and sat, motioning for him to take a seat across from her. "I found... more than I expected."

Jamal's face remained impassive, but she noticed a slight tension in his posture, the way his fingers tapped against the arm of the chair. She had rarely seen him display any nervous habits, and now, watching him, she wondered if he knew more than he was letting on.

"That's a name people don't say out loud," he murmured, barely above a whisper, his gaze dropping to the notebook. "Especially not if they want to stay safe."

Tamika clenched her hands, feeling a surge of determination mixed with fear. "I don't care about safety, Jamal. I care about the truth. People are afraid, and I don't know why, but I can't ignore this anymore. Not after everything I've found."

Jamal let out a long breath, rubbing his temples as if trying to push away the weight of her words. "Tamika, you don't understand what you're getting into. The Circle… it's not just a story. It's real. And it's dangerous."

"Then help me understand," she pressed, leaning forward, her gaze unwavering. "Tell me what the Circle really is. Why people are so terrified of it? Why you're so terrified?"

For a long moment, Jamal said nothing. His eyes drifted toward the shadows dancing along the walls, his face etched with a look she'd never seen before—something deeper than fear. When he finally spoke, his voice was a murmur barely louder than a breath. "The Circle isn't just a group. It's a force. It started as something different, something people trusted. But somewhere along the way, it became something else."

A shiver ran down Tamika's spine at the chill in his tone. She sat back, her curiosity laced with a sense of dread. "What do you mean, it became something else?"

"Power corrupts," Jamal said softly, his voice tinged with regret. "The Circle was meant to protect us, to help us survive. But over time, it became about control, about ensuring that everyone fell in line—whether they wanted to or not."

The weight of his words settled heavily in her mind, and she felt her pulse quicken. She had expected secrets, but this was something more sinister than she had imagined. "Then why do people stay?" she asked, her voice barely above a whisper. "Why do you stay?"

Jamal's gaze met hers, and for the first time, she saw a flicker of vulnerability, a crack in the careful armor he wore. "Because once you're in, there's no way out. The Circle doesn't just let people walk away. They make sure of that."

A chill spread through Tamika, her body tense with the enormity of his words. The Circle wasn't just an organization; it was a trap, a labyrinth with no exit. She could feel the oppressive weight of it pressing down on her, each piece of information adding another link to a chain that was quickly binding her to this dark world.

"Who are they, Jamal?" she asked, her voice trembling. "Who are these people?"

Jamal hesitated, his jaw tightening as he glanced away, as if the question itself was a threat. "They're people who have power, who know how to use it. They control things... things you wouldn't expect. Businesses, institutions, people." He paused, his gaze darkening. "You'd be surprised how many people you know, people you trust, are tied to them."

Her stomach twisted as the implication of his words settled in. She thought of the names she'd uncovered, of the people she had admired and respected within her community. Could they be part of this shadowy organization? Could they really be involved in something so insidious?

"How did you get involved?" she asked, needing to understand his place in all of this.

A bitter smile crossed his face. "I was young. I didn't know any better. They offered me something—a chance to be part of something important, something that mattered. They promised protection, purpose. But I didn't realize the cost."

The silence between them was thick with the weight of his confession. Tamika felt a mixture of anger, pity, and a growing sense of fear. "Is there… any way out?" she asked, though she already feared the answer.

Jamal's face hardened, and he shook his head slowly. "The only way out of the Circle is through it. Once you're marked, once you've seen what they're capable of… there's no turning back. And they make sure you know that."

A cold dread settled over her as she absorbed the gravity of his words. She had thought she was prepared for the truth, but now she realized how naïve she had been. She was dealing with something much larger, much darker than she had anticipated.

"Why are you telling me this?" she asked, her voice barely more than a whisper.

Jamal's gaze softened, a flicker of regret in his eyes. "Because you deserve to know. And because maybe… maybe it's time someone stood up to them."

A spark of hope ignited within her, tempered by the fear that coursed through her veins. She had expected to feel anger, perhaps even betrayal, but instead, there was a sense of purpose building inside her. This wasn't just a story—this was a reckoning.

She looked at Jamal, her resolve hardening. "Then help me," she said, her voice steady. "Help me find a way to expose them."

Jamal hesitated, his gaze searching hers, weighing the risk. "If we do this, there's no turning back. They'll come after us, Tamika. They'll stop at nothing."

"I'm ready," she replied, though a part of her wondered if anyone could truly be ready for what lay ahead.

Jamal sighed, his expression resigned but determined. "Then let's begin."

As he began to speak, filling in the gaps in her knowledge with chilling detail, she felt herself being drawn into a world she could barely comprehend—a place where shadows ruled, and safety was an illusion. The Circle's story was vast, a legacy of secrets and control. And as his voice wove a tale of power, betrayal, and fear, she realized that this was only the beginning.

Chapter 2: Origins in Darkness

The dim glow of the streetlights flickered through the curtains as Tamika settled deeper into her seat, her gaze fixed on Jamal's face. Outside, the city was silent; it was late enough that the usual hum of cars and voices had faded into quiet. But here, in the close confines of her living room, the air was thick with an unspoken tension. Jamal's expression was guarded, and there was a weight in his eyes she hadn't seen before—a sadness that seemed to have settled in over years, not hours.

"It wasn't always like this," he began, his voice barely louder than a whisper. "The Circle, I mean. When it started, it was something… something necessary. A force for protection."

A shiver ran through Tamika, but her curiosity outweighed her fear. She had always suspected that the Circle's roots went deeper than recent rumors, that it hadn't simply sprung up from nowhere to cast its shadow over the community. But hearing Jamal

describe it as "necessary" unsettled her, leaving her feeling as if she was seeing an image through smoke, unable to make out its true form.

"Protection?" Tamika asked, her voice steady despite the emotions churning within her. "Protection from what?"

Jamal's gaze drifted to the window; his eyes distant as if looking back through the years. "You have to understand," he began slowly, "it was a different world back then. Our community was… forgotten. Left to fend for itself. There was violence, corruption, injustice—and no one came to help. People were scared. They were angry, and desperate. Those who were supposed to protect us turned their backs, and soon enough, people started to look out for each other."

Tamika listened intently, feeling a strange sense of recognition in his words. She could almost see it—the broken streets, the shattered neighborhoods, the faces of families trying to piece together lives from the fragments left behind. Her research had given her glimpses of that world but hearing it from Jamal made it feel more real, more immediate.

"They started as a group of community leaders," Jamal continued, his voice soft, almost reverent. "People who had seen it all, who understood how things worked—or didn't work. They were the ones who had spent their lives fighting for change, for justice. But they came together out of necessity, out of a shared understanding that no one else was going to protect us. And so, they decided to create something bigger than themselves. A shield."

Tamika felt her heart pounding as she absorbed his words. She could feel the conviction in Jamal's voice, a conviction that almost made her want to believe in this version of the Circle—a group of protectors, a force created to shield the vulnerable. But even as she listened, she couldn't shake the knowledge of what the Circle had become.

"Who were they?" Tamika asked, her voice a mix of awe and skepticism. "The founders, I mean. Were they people… like you?"

Jamal shook his head, a faint smile touching his lips, but his expression was somber. "Not exactly. They were more… influential. Some were activists, others business owners, people with connections and influence. They knew how to get things done. And they had a vision—a world where our community could thrive, where we could protect each other from those who would tear us down."

Tamika nodded slowly, her mind racing to reconcile this image of the Circle's origins with the fear and violence it had come to represent. "So… what happened?" she asked, barely above a whisper.

Jamal's face darkened, his gaze dropping to the floor. "Power happened," he replied, his voice hardening. "At first, it was just about organizing, about creating a network of support. But then… some of them started to realize how much power they held. And once they tasted that power, it wasn't about protection anymore. It became about control."

A chill ran down Tamika's spine. She could feel the shift in his tone, the bitterness that laced each word.

She could imagine those early days, the way a group of well-meaning individuals might have gradually been seduced by the lure of control.

"Was there... was there a turning point?" she asked, though a part of her feared the answer.

Jamal nodded slowly; his expression haunted. "There were... incidents. People who questioned too much. People who got in the way. The Circle had to decide how far they were willing to go to keep their hold. And they decided... they decided that some sacrifices were necessary."

The word "sacrifices" hung in the air like a dark omen, and Tamika felt her stomach twist. "What kind of sacrifices?" she asked, though every instinct told her she wouldn't want to know.

Jamal's gaze was steady, but she could see the pain in his eyes. "People," he replied quietly. "People who got too close to the truth, or who refused to fall in line. They were... silenced. Erased. The Circle saw it as a way to protect itself, to preserve the cause. But in reality, it was the beginning of the end."

Tamika felt a pang of sadness and anger as she thought of the families, the friends left to wonder what had happened to those who had simply vanished. She thought of the names she'd come across in her research—people who had once been leaders, advocates, voices of change—people who had disappeared without a trace. And all the while, the Circle grew stronger, solidifying its power through fear.

"How did people let this happen?" she asked, her voice filled with anger and disbelief. "How did they not see what was happening?"

Jamal looked at her, a faint sadness in his eyes. "People did see. But they were afraid. The Circle had become so deeply woven into the community, so entangled with everything, that it was impossible to separate it. To fight the Circle was to risk everything—your family, your future. Most people… most people stayed quiet."

A surge of fury coursed through Tamika, an anger that made her hands clench into fists. This wasn't protection—it was a form of oppression, a dark presence that had crept into her community, insidious and silent. And the worst part was that it had all started as something noble.

"But not everyone stayed quiet," she said softly, remembering the names she had uncovered, the people who had dared to speak out.

Jamal's gaze darkened, his expression hardening. "No. Some people tried to resist. They thought they could stand up to the Circle, that they could break free. But the Circle made examples of them. They wanted everyone to see what happened to those who defied them."

Tamika shivered, feeling the coldness of his words settle over her. She could imagine those who had tried to resist, the people who had dared to question the Circle's control, only to disappear, their voices silenced. It was a terrifying reminder of the lengths to which the Circle was willing to go to maintain its power.

"Why are you still here?" she asked, her voice a tremor. "If it's so dangerous… why haven't you left?"

Jamal's expression softened, a hint of vulnerability breaking through his stoic facade. "Because… because I believed in it, once," he said quietly. "I believed the Circle could be a force for good, that it could protect us when no one else would. But now… now I don't know what to believe."

Tamika could see the struggle in his eyes, the war between his loyalty to a cause he had once held dear and the realization that the Circle had become something monstrous.

She took a deep breath, her mind swirling with everything he'd told her. She could feel the weight of the Circle's history pressing down on her, a legacy of shadows and control. This wasn't just a story—it was a warning, a glimpse into a world where power had twisted even the noblest of intentions.

"So what now?" she asked, her voice barely above a whisper. "What do we do with this… with this truth?"

Jamal looked at her, his gaze steady but filled with a quiet determination. "The Circle's power lies in its secrecy; in the fear it instills in people. If we're going to stand a chance, we have to bring its secrets to light."

A spark of hope ignited within her, tempered by the fear that coursed through her veins. She had uncovered a darkness that went deeper than she could have imagined, and now she was bound to it, part of a legacy of silence and control.

But as she looked at Jamal, she felt a renewed sense of purpose. This wasn't just about uncovering the truth—it was about challenging the very foundations of a system that had held her community captive for too long.

"We have to be careful," Jamal warned, his voice filled with a quiet urgency. "The Circle has eyes and ears everywhere. One wrong move, and we could end up like those who came before us."

"I know," Tamika replied, her voice steady. "But I'm willing to take that risk."

A look of respect crossed Jamal's face, and he nodded slowly. "Then we do this together. But we have to move carefully, slowly. We need to understand exactly what we're dealing with before we make any moves."

Tamika nodded, feeling a sense of resolve settle over her. The path ahead was dark and uncertain, but she knew one thing for sure—she couldn't turn back now. She had come too far, seen too much to walk away. The Circle's grip was strong, but she was determined to find a way to break it, to free her community from its hold.

As they sat in silence, the weight of their shared mission settled between them—a silent promise that they would face whatever came their way, together. The Circle had kept its secrets for too long, but now, the truth was beginning to surface. And Tamika was ready to bring its darkness into the light.

Chapter 3: Blood and Betrayal

The air in Tamika's small apartment felt colder as Jamal began to recount the Circle's first true act of violence. He leaned forward, his hands clasped tightly, his eyes fixed on a point somewhere past her shoulder. The quiet stretched between them, thick with unspoken truths. Tamika watched him closely, searching for any flicker of the man she thought she knew. But the person sitting across from her now was someone different—a man marked by secrets, guilt, and a darkness she could barely imagine.

"It wasn't supposed to happen that way," Jamal murmured, his voice strained. His hands tightened, knuckles white, as if holding onto invisible chains. "It was meant to be a statement, a way to show that the community couldn't be ignored anymore. But things… things spiraled out of control."

Tamika leaned forward, her breath catching as she listened. She had found hints of the Circle's past in her research—rumors and fragments of stories that painted a picture of a violent, ruthless organization. But hearing Jamal's firsthand account brought it into painful focus. Each word was like a blade cutting through the facade, revealing something raw and real.

"What happened?" Tamika asked, her voice barely a whisper, as though speaking too loudly might shatter the fragile moment between them.

Jamal took a deep breath, his jaw tight as he prepared himself to relive the night that had haunted him for years. "It started as a protest," he said slowly, his voice tinged with a bitterness that cut through the quiet. "The Circle had planned it carefully, down to the last detail. They wanted to send a message to those in power, to show them that we wouldn't be silent anymore."

He paused, his gaze shifting to the window, his eyes lost in the shadows. "There was so much anger, so much pain. We'd been ignored, pushed aside for too long. People were desperate, ready to do whatever it took to be heard. The protest was supposed to be peaceful, but the Circle... they had other plans."

Tamika's heart pounded as she absorbed his words, each sentence painting a picture of a night filled with tension, fear, and the promise of change. She could almost see it—the crowd gathered in the streets, faces illuminated by streetlights, a sea of voices raised in defiance. But beneath the surface, a darker plan was taking shape, one that would leave scars on her community for years to come.

"Some of the leaders wanted to make a stronger statement," Jamal continued, his voice barely louder than a whisper. "They saw an opportunity to strike fear into the hearts of those who had kept us down. They planned an ambush, a way to make sure our voices were heard—no matter the cost."

A chill ran down Tamika's spine as she imagined the scene, the tension building as the protestors stood united, unaware of the storm brewing around them. She could almost hear the shouts, the chants, the surge of energy that filled the air. But beneath it all, there was an undercurrent of danger, a sense of foreboding that made her stomach twist.

"It started with a single spark," Jamal said, his eyes dark with the memory. "Someone threw a bottle, then another. And suddenly, the crowd was a wave, crashing against the barriers, fueled by years of anger and frustration. It was chaos—people shouting, pushing, fighting. And then... then the Circle made their move."

Tamika held her breath, her mind racing to keep up with the images he painted. She could almost see the faces in the crowd, their expressions shifting from hope to fear as the protest descended into chaos. It was a scene of turmoil, of raw emotion spilling over as the crowd's collective pain erupted in a wave of violence.

"The Circle had planned it all," Jamal continued, his voice tight. "They knew that if they pushed hard enough, people would break. They knew that fear was a powerful tool, that once it took hold, it would be impossible to shake."

He paused, his gaze dropping to the floor. "But things went further than anyone expected. People were hurt... people died. Innocent lives, caught in the crossfire. And the Circle… they saw it as a necessary cost."

Tamika felt a knot form in her stomach as she listened, the horror of his words sinking in. She could see the scene clearly in her mind—people running, shouting, their faces twisted in fear and confusion as the night descended into chaos. And amid the turmoil, the Circle stood, a silent force, orchestrating the violence from the shadows.

"But it wasn't just a statement, was it?" she asked softly, her voice trembling. "It was… it was a warning."

Jamal nodded slowly, his expression haunted. "Yes. A warning to anyone who dared to stand against them. The Circle had found its power, and they weren't going to let it go. They saw that fear was a way to control, to keep people in line. And from that night on, they became something else—something darker, something ruthless."

A heavy silence settled over the room as Tamika processed his words. She felt a surge of anger mixed with sorrow, a wrenching sense of injustice for those whose lives had been torn apart by the Circle's ambitions. She had always sensed that the organization held a sinister power, but hearing it confirmed in such brutal detail was something else entirely.

"How could they... how could they justify this?" she asked, her voice filled with disbelief and disgust.

Jamal looked at her, his eyes heavy with regret. "They convinced themselves it was for the greater good, that the ends justified the means. They told themselves that the fear they instilled was necessary to protect our community, to keep it strong. But in reality, it was about control. They wanted to keep everyone in line."

Tamika shook her head, unable to understand the twisted logic that had allowed the Circle to justify such violence. "But they weren't protecting anyone," she said, her voice breaking. "They were... they were controlling people, using fear as a weapon."

Jamal's face tightened, a flicker of shame crossing his features. "I know," he said quietly. "But back then,

I… I didn't see it that way. I thought… I thought we were fighting for something, that we were building a future where we could be safe, where we could stand tall."

He paused, his gaze dropping to the floor. "But now… now I see the cost. I see the lives we destroyed, the families torn apart by our actions. And I wonder… was it worth it?"

The question hung in the air, a painful reminder of the moral cost that had come with the Circle's rise to power. Tamika felt a pang of empathy for Jamal, a man who had once believed in a cause that had betrayed him. She could see the weight of his guilt, the way it had carved lines into his face, leaving him haunted by the choices he had made.

"What about the people who tried to stand up to them?" she asked, her voice barely a whisper. "The ones who didn't agree with the Circle's methods?"

Jamal's expression darkened. "They didn't last long. The Circle had a way of… dealing with dissent. They made sure that anyone who questioned them was silenced. Some of them disappeared, others were... persuaded to fall in line."

The cold finality of his words sent a shiver through her. She thought of the names she had found, the people who had once been leaders, advocates, voices for justice in the community—people who had vanished without a trace, leaving only whispers and unanswered questions. The Circle had become a force that crushed anyone who dared to stand in its way.

Tamika looked at Jamal, a mix of fear and anger bubbling within her. "How are you still part of this?" she demanded, her voice trembling. "How can you live with it?"

Jamal's face tightened, and for a moment, she thought he wouldn't answer. But then he looked at her, his eyes raw with regret. "Because it's all I know," he said softly. "I thought about leaving once, after that first protest. I thought about walking away, trying to build a life outside of the Circle. But the Circle... they made sure I remembered the cost."

"What cost?" she asked, her voice a whisper.

"They came to my house one night," he replied, his voice barely audible. "They told me they'd heard I was having second thoughts, that I was thinking of breaking the code. They reminded me that loyalty was everything… that there was no room for doubt."

He swallowed hard, his gaze distant. "They mentioned my family, my friends. They told me that if I so much as breathed a word to anyone outside the Circle, they would pay the price."

Tamika felt a surge of horror as she listened, the implications of his words settling over her like a 10lb weight. She could see the fear in his eyes, the memory of that night etched into his face, a scar he could never erase. The Circle had bound him to its will, trapping him in a prison he could never escape.

"Why are you telling me this?" she asked, her voice barely more than a whisper.

Jamal looked at her, a flicker of something like hope in his eyes. "Because you deserve to know the truth. And because maybe… maybe it's time the Circle's secrets started to come to light."

A spark of hope ignited within her, tempered by the fear that coursed through her veins. She had expected to feel anger, maybe even betrayal, but instead, there was a sense of purpose building inside her. This was more than a story. The Circle's history was filled with shadows, but perhaps, just perhaps, there was still a chance for change.

As she sat in silence, absorbing everything he had shared, she realized that she was no longer just an observer. By learning the Circle's secrets, she had become part of its story, bound to its fate in ways she hadn't anticipated. And she knew, with a certainty that frightened her.

Chapter 4: The Code of Silence

The room was silent, the weight of Jamal's words lingering like a shadow that stretched across the walls. Tamika sat on the edge of the couch, her mind reeling as she tried to comprehend everything she'd learned. The Circle wasn't just an organization—it was a force that permeated every corner of her community, weaving fear and silence into the lives of those it touched.

Jamal's gaze dropped to his hands, which were clenched tightly in his lap, the knuckles white from the pressure. She waited, sensing there was more he had yet to reveal. Finally, he looked up, his eyes dark and haunted.

"You asked me once why people stay in the Circle," he said quietly, his voice barely louder than a whisper. "The answer is simple. They stay because they have no choice."

Tamika frowned, her curiosity tinged with fear. She had sensed this truth in the way people around her kept their heads down, the way her questions about the Circle were met with guarded looks and whispered warnings. But hearing it confirmed by someone on the inside made her pulse quicken.

"What do you mean... no choice?" she asked, her voice trembling.

Jamal's eyes met hers, and she saw something painful in his eyes. "The Circle has a code of silence, an unbreakable rule that binds every member. Once you're in, you're bound to that code for life. If you try to leave, if you speak out... they make sure you pay the price."

Tamika's stomach twisted as she listened, the weight of his words pressing down on her. She had known, somewhere deep inside, that the Circle's power went beyond simple loyalty, but this—this was something else entirely. It was a trap, a prison without walls, where silence was the price of survival.

"How... how do they enforce it?" she asked, dreading the answer.

Jamal's expression darkened, his jaw tightening as if he was steeling himself for what he was about to say.

"They enforce it with fear. They make examples of people—people who thought they could walk away or speak out. And they don't just punish the person; they go after their family, their friends, anyone who might be close to them. It's a message to the rest of us, a reminder of what loyalty truly costs."

A chill ran down Tamika's spine. This wasn't just about loyalty—it was about control, a manipulation so deep that it left no room for rebellion, no space for escape.

"So... people just disappear?" she asked, her voice trembling.

Jamal nodded, his expression grim. "Disappear, silenced... erased. The Circle has connections everywhere, people who can make things happen, make people vanish without a trace. And the worst part is, no one questions it. They've created an atmosphere where people don't dare ask too many questions. It's easier to look away, to pretend you don't see the warning signs, than to risk your own life by digging too deep."

Tamika felt a surge of anger mixed with fear. The image of a community held hostage by silence, by the constant threat of violence, made her heart ache. This wasn't protection; it was oppression, a darkness that had seeped into the very fabric of her world. And the worst part was that it had become so normalized, so ingrained, that people accepted it as part of life.

"That's not loyalty," she said softly, her voice filled with a mixture of disbelief and disgust. "That's fear."

Jamal's face tightened. "I know," he said quietly. "But when you're inside it, when you're part of something like this, you start to see things differently. You start to believe that maybe this is the only way to survive, that maybe silence is the only thing keeping you safe."

"But what about… what about those who stay silent?" she asked, her voice filled with a mixture of anger and despair. "The ones who know the truth but choose to look the other way?"

Jamal's gaze softened, "Most people…know what the Circle is capable of, and they know that one wrong move could mean losing everything. So, they keep their heads down, follow the rules, and hope that they don't end up on the wrong side of the Circle's wrath."

The weight of his words pressed down on her, filling her with a sense of hopelessness she hadn't anticipated. This wasn't just an organization; it was a shadow that stretched across her entire community, a force that demanded obedience at any cost.

The road ahead would be difficult, filled with danger and uncertainty, but she was prepared to face it. This was more than a fight for justice—it was a fight for freedom, a chance to break the chains that had held her community captive for so long. And she was determined to see it through, no matter the cost.

Chapter 5: The Power Struggle

The evening shadows lengthened as Tamika sat across from Jamal, processing everything she had learned. The Circle's reach was vast and ruthless, its members bound by an unbreakable code of silence. But tonight, Jamal was about to reveal something unexpected—something that shattered her image of the Circle as a single, unified force.

"The Circle... it's not what most people think," he said, his voice quiet but filled with a bitter edge. "It's not a single entity, not anymore. It's made up of people—people with different agendas, different visions of what they want the Circle to be. And they're willing to do whatever it takes to get there."

Tamika leaned forward, her heart pounding with a mixture of curiosity and dread. She had always imagined the Circle as a monolithic organization, its members united by a shared purpose. But the idea of factions within the Circle—factions led by powerful individuals fighting for control—painted a far more dangerous picture.

"What do you mean, different agendas?" she asked, her voice laced with tension.

Jamal sighed, rubbing his temples as if the memories physically pained him. "There are factions within the Circle. Some leaders think the Circle should stay in the shadows, pulling strings quietly from behind the scenes. They believe in fear as a subtle tool, something to keep people in line without drawing too much attention. Others... others want something more public. They believe fear isn't enough—they want people to know who's in charge."

Goosebumps rose on her skin as she imagined the kinds of people who would see fear and control as mere tools, weapons to be wielded for personal power. The Circle wasn't just an organization—it was a battlefield, where loyalty was fleeting, and everyone was a potential enemy.

"There's always someone looking to climb the ladder, to take control," Jamal continued, his voice thick with bitterness. "They'll do whatever it takes. Blackmail, threats, even violence... nothing is off-limits."

Tamika felt a wave of dread wash over her. This wasn't just a group united by a single cause; it was a web of alliances and betrayals, a shifting landscape where power was everything and trust was a luxury few could afford.

"Have you... have you seen this happen?" she asked, her voice barely above a whisper.

Jamal's looked down, "More times than I care to remember. People who thought they were safe, who thought they had allies... only to find out their so-called friends were willing to sell them out for a chance at power. I've seen people betrayed by those closest to them, sacrificed for someone else's ambition."

He paused, the memory haunted him. "There was a man once, someone I respected. He was one of the few who actually believed in the Circle's original mission, in protecting the community. But he... he got in the way. He questioned the methods, the violence, the secrecy. And the others... they turned on him."

Tamika felt her heart twist as she listened. She imagined the pain of betrayal, the feeling of being surrounded by enemies disguised as friends. This man, whoever he was, had dared to challenge the Circle's methods, to stand up for what he believed in. But in the world of the Circle, principles were dangerous, and loyalty was a fragile thing.

"What happened to him?" she asked softly, almost fearing the answer.

Jamal had anger flashing in his eyes. "They made an example of him. They took everything—his connections, his business, even his family. By the time they were done, he was a shell of the man he had once been. And when he finally disappeared, no one dared to ask where he went. It was a warning to the rest of us, a reminder that loyalty to the Circle meant loyalty to the people in power, no matter what."

Tamika was overcome with a mix of fury and grief, a wrenching sense of injustice for this man who had been torn apart by the very organization he had once believed in. She could see the cruelty, the way the Circle had manipulated and discarded him, another sacrifice on the altar of ambition.

Jamal looked at her, a faint, bitter smile crossing his lips. "Because power is seductive, Tamika. It has a way of pulling people in, convincing them they're invincible, that they can change things from the inside. And by the time they realize the truth—it's too late."

He paused, his eyes dropped to the floor. "The Circle has a way of... making you believe that you're part of something bigger, that you're important. And for some people, that's enough. They're willing to turn a blind eye, to ignore the corruption, as long as they get to keep their power."

Tamika shook her head, her hands clenched in anger. "This isn't about loyalty or protection. It's about greed, ambition... control."

Jamal's face softened, a trace of sympathy in his eyes. "I know. But people don't always see it that way, especially when they're inside. They see what they want to see. They believe the lie because it's easier than facing the truth."

He leaned forward, his gaze intense. "If we're going to take them down, we have to be careful. We have to understand the players, the alliances, the power struggles. One wrong move, and they'll come after us with everything they've got."

Tamika nodded, feeling a sense of resolve settle over her. This wasn't just a fight for justice—it was a fight for survival, a battle against an enemy that knew no mercy. She could feel the weight of the Circle's power pressing down on her, but she refused to back down. This was her community, her people, and she was determined to protect them from the darkness that had claimed so many lives.

"Then we start with what we know," she said, her voice steady. "We map out the players, the alliances. We figure out who's in control, who's loyal, and who's a threat. And then… we find a way to bring them down."

Jamal nodded, a flicker of admiration in his eyes. "It won't be easy, Tamika. These people… they're ruthless. They'll do whatever it takes to protect their power. They won't hesitate to destroy us if they see us as a threat."

"I know," she replied, her voice filled with determination. "But I'm ready to take that risk. They've taken enough from us. It's time to fight back."

As they sat in silence, the weight of their shared mission settled between them—a silent promise that they would face whatever came their way, together. The Circle had kept its secrets for too long, but now, the truth was beginning to surface. And Tamika was ready to bring its darkness into the light.

Chapter 6: Collateral Damage

The clock on the wall ticked loudly in the silence, each second stretching as Tamika's heart raced. She sat across from Jamal, the weight of their conversation pressing down on her like an invisible force. She had agreed to fight the Circle, to uncover its secrets and expose its web of fear and control. But now, as she listened to Jamal reveal yet another disturbing truth, she felt her resolve waver.

"You need to understand something, Tamika," Jamal said quietly, his gaze fixed on her, his face shadowed in the dim light of the room. "The Circle doesn't just control people through threats and power. They also use… punishment."

"Punishment?" she repeated, her stomach twisting at the word.

Jamal nodded slowly. "They call it 'collateral damage.' It's a way to send a message, to remind everyone of the price of betrayal. They don't just go after the person who defies them—they go after everyone that person cares about."

Tamika's blood ran cold as she absorbed his words. She had suspected that the Circle was ruthless, that it used fear to keep people in line, but hearing it confirmed, understanding that it wasn't just an unspoken rule but an official practice, shook her to her core. "So they... punish families? Friends?"

Jamal nodded, his expression somber. "Anyone close to the person. It's how they ensure loyalty. Once you're marked as a traitor or even as a 'risk,' they go after everything you hold dear. They make sure you know that if you defy them, you're not the only one who will pay the price."

Tamika felt a surge of nausea, her mind racing as she thought of the countless families who must have been torn apart, the loved ones forced to suffer for one person's supposed "disloyalty." This was more than just control—it was cruelty, a calculated method to ensure compliance by preying on the most vulnerable parts of a person's life.

"They don't even need a reason sometimes," Jamal continued, his voice tinged with bitterness. "Sometimes it's enough for them to think you're a threat. They've targeted people who just happened to be in the wrong place at the wrong time, people who saw too much or asked the wrong questions. And once they're marked as collateral, they're… they're disposable."

Tamika's heart raced; her hands clenched tightly in her lap. This was a new level of horror, a revelation that made her feel as if she were drowning in the darkness surrounding her community. The Circle was a predator, feeding off the fear and suffering of innocent people, using their loved ones as leverage to ensure silence.

"Do you know anyone… who was a victim of this?" she asked softly, her voice trembling.

Jamal's face darkened, and for a moment, he looked away, as if reliving a memory, he had long tried to bury. "Yes," he said finally, his voice barely above a whisper. "There was a man named Marcus. He owned a small shop, a place people trusted, a place where people went to find a bit of comfort in a world filled with chaos. Marcus was... a good man, one of the few people who stood up to the Circle."

Tamika listened, her heart aching as she pictured this man, this innocent person who had dared to defy the darkness surrounding him.

"He had a family," Jamal continued, his voice heavy with grief. "A wife, two kids. He was a good father, a good husband. But he made the mistake of asking too many questions, of refusing to let the Circle dictate his life. And so... they made an example of him."

Tamika's stomach twisted as she imagined the scene, the horror that must have unfolded as Marcus's life was torn apart. "What did they do to him?"

"They destroyed everything," Jamal replied, his voice tight. "They spread rumors, turned people against him. They ruined his business, drove his family into debt. And then... they disappeared him."

"Disappeared him?", Tamika asked.

Jamal nodded, his gaze dark with pain. "One night, he just... vanished. No one saw him again. His family was left with nothing, and no one dared to ask questions. It was a message—a reminder of what happens to those who defy the Circle."

Tamika felt a surge of anger, a burning fury that made her hands tremble. This wasn't just a story; it was a nightmare, a world where innocence was sacrificed on the altar of control, where lives were destroyed without a second thought.

"His family... what happened to them?" she asked, her voice filled with sorrow.

Jamal's face tightened, and he looked away, his jaw clenched. "They were forced to leave, to disappear themselves. They couldn't stay in the community, not after everything that had happened. They left in the dead of night, with nothing but the clothes on their backs. And the Circle made sure they would never come back."

Tamika felt a pang of sadness and anger as she imagined the shattered family, the lives destroyed by the Circle's cruelty. She thought of the countless others who must have suffered the same fate, people who had been forced into silence, their voices silenced by fear.

"This is more than just control," she said softly, her voice trembling with rage. "This is... it's evil."

Jamal nodded, filled with a mixture of anger and sorrow. "I know. But that's why we have to fight, Tamika. That's why we have to bring the truth to light, no matter the cost. Because if we don't... this will never end."

Tamika took a deep breath, her resolve hardening. She had already agreed to fight, to uncover the Circle's secrets and expose its darkness. But now, after hearing about Marcus, after understanding the true extent of the Circle's cruelty, she felt a renewed sense of purpose. This wasn't just a battle for justice—it was a battle for redemption, a chance to honor the lives that had been destroyed by the Circle's merciless pursuit of power.

"We need to find proof," she said, her voice steady. "Evidence that shows what they've done, that exposes the full extent of their cruelty. And then... we take it to the people."

Jamal nodded, a glimmer of hope in his eyes. "It won't be easy. The Circle has eyes and ears everywhere. They'll know if we're getting close, and they'll do whatever it takes to stop us."

"I'm not afraid," she replied, though a part of her knew that wasn't entirely true. The thought of going up against an enemy as powerful as the Circle filled her with fear, but it was a fear she was willing to face.

As they sat in silence, the weight of their shared mission settled between them—a promise to honor the lives that had been lost, to bring justice to those who had been silenced. The Circle had thrived on fear and control, but now, Tamika was ready to stand against it, to challenge the darkness that had claimed so many lives.

The road ahead would be dangerous, filled with uncertainty and risk, but she was determined to see it through. This was more than just a fight—it was a chance to reclaim her community, to break the chains of fear and bring the Circle's reign of terror to an end.

And as she looked at Jamal, she knew that they would face whatever came their way, together. The Circle's power was vast, but their resolve was stronger. And she was ready to bring its darkness into the light.

Chapter 7: The Grip of Fear

The quiet streets outside Tamika's window seemed peaceful under the cover of night, but she knew that peace was an illusion. Within the walls of her small apartment, shadows loomed, the darkness heavier than ever. She sat beside Jamal, the weight of their shared purpose hanging thickly between them. They were surrounded by secrets, by lies that had kept the Circle in power for so long. But as Jamal's latest revelation settled over her, she felt her world closing in.

"They're everywhere, Tamika," he said, his voice barely a whisper, as if even the walls had ears. "The Circle has eyes and ears in every corner of this community. People you wouldn't suspect—neighbors, shopkeepers, even close friends—some of them are informants, passing information back to the Circle."

Tamika's stomach twisted at the thought, her pulse racing as the implications sank in. The idea that her community, her neighbors, might be part of the very force that had terrorized her people was terrifying. It meant that no one was safe, that trust was a fragile, dangerous thing.

"How can they... how can they convince people to do this?" she asked, her voice tinged with disbelief and disgust.

Jamal sighed, running a hand through his hair. "The Circle doesn't give them much choice. Some of these people, they're being blackmailed, threatened. The Circle digs up their secrets, their weaknesses, and then uses those as leverage. Others... others do it for power, for protection, believing that being on the inside makes them safe."

Tamika felt a surge of anger and sadness as she listened. Her heart ached for those who were trapped, forced to betray their community to protect their own lives. But for the ones who chose to inform willingly, who sold out their neighbors for a taste of power, she felt only contempt.

"So we can't trust anyone," she said, her voice barely above a whisper.

Jamal nodded slowly. "We have to assume that anyone could be a risk. One wrong word, one slip-up, and they'll know what we're planning. They'll know we're coming after them."

Tamika's mind raced, her pulse quickening as she considered the gravity of their situation. This wasn't just a fight against a faceless enemy; this was a battle against a network that had seeped into every part of her life, a web of secrets and lies that had turned friends into potential enemies.

"But there has to be someone we can trust," she insisted, a trace of desperation in her voice. "Someone who's loyal, who's willing to fight with us."

Jamal hesitated, his gaze dropping to the floor. "There are people… people who want to see the Circle fall. But finding them, knowing who's truly on our side—it's a gamble. If we make one wrong move, we could expose ourselves before we're ready."

Tamika nodded, feeling the weight of his words press down on her. She knew that their mission was dangerous, that every step they took brought them closer to the Circle's wrath. But the idea of facing this fight alone, without allies, filled her with a sense of dread.

"So... what do we do?" she asked, her voice trembling slightly.

Jamal looked at her, his eyes filled with a quiet resolve. "We move carefully. We watch, we listen. We don't make any moves until we're certain. And above all, we stay in the shadows. The Circle thrives on fear, on knowing that they control everything. If we're going to take them down, we have to play their game, at least for now."

Tamika took a deep breath, nodding slowly. She knew that he was right, that their only chance at survival was to outwit the Circle, to move silently and strike when they least expected it. But the thought of living in constant fear, of watching her every word and action, was exhausting. She could feel the tension building within her, the weight of her mission pressing down on her shoulders.

As the silence settled between them, Tamika thought of her friends, her family—people she had known her whole life, people she had trusted without question.

Could they really be part of this network of informants, reporting her every move back to the Circle? The thought was unbearable, but she knew she couldn't ignore it. This was the reality she was facing, a reality where loyalty was a rare, fragile thing.

Just as she was about to speak, a sound outside her window caught her attention—a soft rustling, barely audible but unmistakable. Her heart raced, and she exchanged a quick glance with Jamal. He moved silently to the window, peeking through a small gap in the curtains.

"What is it?" she whispered, her voice barely audible.

Jamal's face was tense as he peered outside, his gaze sharp and alert. "Someone's out there," he murmured. "Watching."

Tamika's heart pounded, her mind racing as she considered the implications. Had they already been discovered? Was the Circle already aware of their plans?

Jamal turned back to her, his expression serious. "We need to move. We can't stay here. If they're watching us, it's only a matter of time before they make a move."

Tamika nodded, grabbing her bag and slipping on her jacket, her mind focused on survival. She felt a surge of adrenaline, a fierce determination to escape before it was too late. She had come too far, learned too much to let the Circle silence her now.

They slipped out the back door, moving quietly through the shadows, their footsteps barely audible as they made their way down the narrow alley. The night was dark, the streetlights casting long, eerie shadows that seemed to follow them, like silent witnesses to their escape.

As they moved, Tamika couldn't shake the feeling of being watched, the sense that unseen eyes were tracking their every step. The Circle's reach was everywhere, its influence woven into the very fabric of her community. She knew that every corner, every alley could hold a threat, an informant ready to report back to the Circle.

Finally, they reached a small, secluded park on the edge of the neighborhood. They stopped, catching their breath, the silence around them thick with tension.

"What now?" she asked, her voice barely above a whisper.

Jamal looked around, his gaze scanning the darkness. "We lay low for now. We need to find a safe place, somewhere the Circle won't think to look. And then... we plan our next move."

Tamika nodded, her mind racing with a mixture of fear and determination. She knew that the path ahead would be dangerous, that every step brought them closer to the Circle's wrath. But she was willing to face that danger, to confront the darkness that had held her community captive for so long.

As they sat in the shadows, Tamika felt a surge of resolve. This was more than just a fight for justice—it was a battle for freedom, a chance to break the chains of fear and bring the Circle's reign of terror to an end. She was ready to face whatever came her way, to challenge the darkness and bring its secrets to light.

And as she looked at Jamal, she knew that she wasn't alone in this fight. Together, they would face the Circle, confront its power, and expose its lies. The road ahead would be long and dangerous, but she was ready to see it through.

Chapter 8: Recruitment and Manipulation

The cramped, dimly lit room was silent except for the faint hum of a nearby streetlight. Tamika glanced around, her mind buzzing with tension and adrenaline. She and Jamal had spent hours moving through backstreets and quiet alleys, avoiding the main roads and staying out of sight. Now they sat in the apartment of a former classmate, hoping they were far enough away to avoid the Circle's prying eyes and ears.

The apartment was sparse, with only a few worn-out chairs and a rickety table in the center, but it was safe—for now. The man sitting across from her was Malik, someone she hadn't seen in years. He had been an idealist in his youth, someone who had always spoken out about injustice, and now he was listening intently as she explained her plan.

"You really think you can take them down?" Malik asked, his voice a mixture of skepticism and awe. "The Circle isn't just a gang or a group of thugs. They're woven into every part of this community."

Tamika took a deep breath, her gaze unwavering. "I know it's dangerous, Malik. But we can't let fear stop us. They've hurt too many people, destroyed too many lives. If we don't stand up to them, who will?"

Malik sighed, leaning back in his chair, his. "People are scared, Tamika. They've seen what the Circle can do. They've lost family, friends... no one wants to risk becoming the next target."

Jamal, who had been silent up to this point, leaned forward, his voice low but firm. "This isn't about bravery, Malik. It's about survival. The Circle will keep tightening its grip unless we push back. We're not asking people to fight recklessly, but to be part of something that can make a difference."

Malik looked between them. He was visibly torn, caught between the desire to stand up for what was right and the instinct to protect himself. Tamika understood his fear—it was the same fear that had kept so many people silent. But she also knew that if they didn't break that silence, nothing would ever change.

"Think about your family, Malik," she said softly, her voice filled with quiet conviction. "Think about your kids, the kind of future you want for them. Do you really want them growing up in a world where fear and corruption are normal? Where the Circle decides who lives and who suffers?"

Malik's jaw tightened, and he looked away, his fists clenching at his sides. She could see the internal struggle etched across his face, the anger simmering beneath the surface. Finally, he let out a long breath and nodded.

"All right," he said, his voice barely a whisper. "I'm in. But we must be smart about this. If they get wind of what we're doing…"

"They won't," Jamal replied quickly. "We'll be careful. And we'll move slowly. We're going to build a network, quietly, with people we know we can trust."

A sense of relief washed over Tamika, mingling with the fear that had been building inside her. She knew that their fight was only beginning, that the Circle would stop at nothing to protect its power. But having an ally, even just one, gave her a renewed sense of hope.

The three of them spent the next hour strategizing, discussing the best way to approach others who might be willing to join their cause. They made a list of people who had suffered at the hands of the Circle, individuals who might be looking for a chance to strike back. Some were old friends, others were strangers, but they all had one thing in common: a desire for change.

As the clock ticked past midnight, Malik walked them to the door, his expression serious. "I'll start talking to people, see who's willing to listen. But you need to be careful. The Circle… they have a way of knowing things before anyone else does. They've got informants, spies—people who are willing to sell out their neighbors for a little extra protection."

Tamika nodded, her heart heavy with the weight of his words. She knew that building a network of allies would be risky, that each new recruit increased the chance of betrayal. But they had no other choice. If they wanted to bring down the Circle, they needed people who were willing to take a stand.

"Thank you, Malik," she said, her voice filled with gratitude. "We'll be in touch."

They left the apartment quietly, slipping back into the shadows of the night. Tamika felt a renewed sense of determination, but also a deep-seated fear that gnawed at the edges of her resolve. The Circle was powerful, and its reach extended into places she couldn't see. She and Jamal were taking a dangerous path, one that could easily end in disaster.

As they walked, Jamal's expression remained tense, his eyes scanning the empty streets. "We have to be careful about who we trust," he said softly, his voice barely audible. "The Circle has a way of finding out things. They manipulate people, use their weaknesses against them. And they don't care who they hurt in the process."

Tamika nodded, her mind racing as she thought of the people she hoped to recruit. She knew that some would be willing to stand with her, that they shared her anger and desire for change. But others might be too afraid, too broken by the Circle's power to risk defying them.

"Do you think Malik will come through?" she asked, her voice tinged with uncertainty.

Jamal shrugged; his expression guarded. "I think he wants to help. But wanting something and being able to follow through on it… those are two different things."

She understood what he meant. Malik had been sincere in his promise to help, but she couldn't shake the feeling that his fear might get the best of him. The Circle's power was too vast, too deeply entrenched in the community, and she knew that anyone who joined their cause would be risking everything.

They walked in silence for a few more minutes, the weight of their mission pressing down on them. Tamika felt a surge of determination, a fierce resolve to see this through no matter the cost. She had come too far, seen too much to turn back now.

But just as they were about to turn the corner toward her apartment, a figure stepped out from the shadows, blocking their path. Tamika's heart skipped a beat, her mind racing as she took in the man's face.

It was someone she knew, someone she had trusted.

"Jamal, Tamika," he said, his voice calm but with an edge of something darker. "We need to talk."

Tamika glanced at Jamal, her pulse quickening as she recognized the man—one of her neighbors, someone she had known for years. The shock of seeing him there, standing in the shadows with an unreadable expression, sent a chill down her spine.

"What... what are you doing here?" she asked, her voice barely above a whisper.

The man looked at her, his gaze steady. "You think you're the only ones who want to fight back?" he asked, his voice low and filled with a strange intensity. "You think you're the only ones who have been hurt by the Circle?"

Tamika felt a surge of relief mixed with caution. She wanted to believe him, to believe that he was there to join them, but something in his tone made her wary.

"I've been watching you," he continued, his gaze shifting between her and Jamal. "And I know what you're planning. You're trying to bring down the Circle."

Tamika's heart pounded as she listened, her mind racing. She hadn't realized anyone had been watching her, let alone someone so close to home. But now, as she looked into his eyes, she saw a flicker of something familiar—anger, desperation, a hunger for change.

"Are you with us?" she asked, her voice steady despite the fear gnawing at her.

The man paused; his gaze intense. "I'm with you," he said finally. "But you need to know something. The Circle… they're already suspicious. They've been watching, listening. They know that something's happening, that people are talking."

Tamika's stomach twisted with fear, but she kept her gaze steady. "Then we need to move quickly," she replied. "Before they have a chance to stop us."

The man nodded; his expression grim. "I'll help you. But you need to be careful. There are people in this community who will turn on you in an instant if it means protecting themselves."

She felt a surge of determination as she listened, a fierce resolve to see this through no matter the cost. The Circle had kept her community in fear for too long, and she was ready to do whatever it took to bring its secrets to light.

As they stood in the shadows, the three of them sharing a silent pact, Tamika knew that their mission had just become even more dangerous. The Circle was watching, waiting, ready to strike at the first sign of rebellion. But she also knew that they weren't alone, that there were others who shared her anger, her desire for justice.

The road ahead would be filled with danger, with betrayal and sacrifice. But she was ready to face it. She would bring the Circle's reign of fear to an end—no matter what it took.

Chapter 9: The Justification of Violence

The air was thick with tension as Tamika and Jamal slipped into a quiet, abandoned building on the edge of town, a place they had begun to use as a temporary meeting spot. The building was dusty, the windows covered in grime, but it was safe—for now. Tamika's mind raced as she thought about everything they had planned, everything they were risking.

Jamal stood by the window, his body tense. He had been unusually quiet all evening, his usual confidence replaced by something darker, something that made Tamika's heart ache. She wanted to reach out, to reassure him, but a part of her knew that words wouldn't be enough.

After a long silence, he turned to her, his expression solemn. "Tamika, we need to talk about what comes next."

She nodded, crossing her arms as she leaned against the wall. "I know. We're close to exposing the Circle's secrets, but we have to be careful. If we're not careful, we'll end up like the others."

Jamal shook his head, his gaze sharp. "I'm not talking about the risks, Tamika. I'm talking about… what we're willing to do to win this fight."

She had sensed Jamal's growing frustration, his anger at the Circle's stronghold on their community. But now, as she looked into his eyes, she saw something else—a fierceness, a desperation that frightened her.

"What are you saying, Jamal?" she asked.

He sighed, running a hand through his hair or lack thereof. "I'm saying that the Circle doesn't play fair. They use violence, threats, fear—they'll do anything to keep people in line. And if we're going to have a chance, we might have to fight fire with fire."

Tamika's heart pounded as she listened, her mind racing. She had always believed that their fight was about justice, about exposing the Circle's corruption and bringing its members to light. But now, as she heard Jamal's words, she realized that he was talking about something else entirely.

"You're saying we should use violence?" she asked, a note of disbelief in her voice.

Jamal's jaw tightened, and he looked away. "I'm saying that sometimes, violence is the only language people like them understand. The Circle has controlled this community for years, and they won't let go without a fight. If we want to make a real difference, we might have to do things we're... not comfortable with."

Tamika felt a rush as she listened. She had always known that their mission would be dangerous, that they would be forced to make sacrifices. But she hadn't expected this, hadn't expected Jamal to suggest crossing a line she wasn't sure she could cross.

"Jamal, we're trying to make things better," she said, her voice trembling. "If we use violence, we become like them... then what's the point? We'll be no different than the Circle."

He looked at her, "The point, Tamika, is to win. To take back our community, to give people hope again. If that means getting our hands dirty, then maybe that's what we have to do."

The words hung between them, heavy with unspoken truths. Tamika could see the desperation in his eyes, the anger that simmered just beneath the surface. She knew that he had lost people to the Circle, that he carried wounds that hadn't healed. But she also knew that if they gave in to violence, if they became the very thing they were fighting against, they would lose more than just the battle—they would lose themselves.

"Jamal, this isn't just about winning," she said softly, her voice filled with a quiet determination. "It's about doing what's right. If we start using violence, if we justify hurting people to get what we want... then we're no better than them."

He looked away, his jaw tight. She could see the struggle etched across his face, the conflict between his desire for justice and his anger at everything the Circle had taken from him. For a long moment, he said nothing, his silence a painful reminder of the darkness that lay within them both.

Finally, he spoke, his voice barely a whisper. "Maybe you're right. Maybe we can't fight them that way. But if they come after us, if they try to hurt us or the people we care about… I won't stand by and let it happen. I'll do whatever it takes to protect you, to protect everyone who's helping us."

Tamika nodded slowly, understanding the weight of his words. She knew that their mission was dangerous, that they would be forced to make difficult choices. But she also knew that if they let fear and anger drive them, they would lose everything that mattered.

"We're going to win this fight, Jamal," she said softly, her voice filled with a quiet strength. "But we're going to do it our way. We're going to bring the truth to light, and we're going to make sure people see the Circle for what it really is. We don't have to become them to defeat them."

He looked at her, and for a moment, the tension between them faded. She could see the flicker of hope in his eyes, a reminder of the man she had come to trust, the man who had stood by her side through everything.

"Okay," he said finally, his voice barely audible. "We'll do it your way. But if things go south, if they try to hurt you…" He paused, his jaw tightening. "I won't stand by and let it happen. Not again."

Tamika nodded, a rush of gratitude washing over her. She knew that their fight was far from over, that the path ahead would be filled with danger and uncertainty. But she also knew that she wasn't alone, that she had someone by her side who was willing to risk everything for the chance to make things right.

As they left the building, slipping back into the shadows of the night, Tamika felt a renewed sense of purpose. She knew that the Circle wouldn't give up easily, that they would fight to protect their power. But she was ready, determined to face whatever came her way.

The road ahead would be long and dangerous, but she was prepared to walk it. She would bring the Circle's reign of fear to an end—not through violence, but through truth. And she knew, with a certainty that filled her heart, that together, she and Jamal could make a difference.

Chapter 10: Seeds of Rebellion

The air in the abandoned warehouse was thick with dust, the scent of damp wood and rusted metal filling Tamika's nostrils as she and Jamal entered. The space was vast and empty, the perfect place for a gathering that had to be kept hidden. She glanced around, heart pounding, hoping they'd gone undetected. Tonight was their first meeting with the allies Malik had gathered. She knew that if the Circle caught wind of this, it would be over before they even began.

One by one, people trickled in, each arrival heightening the tension in the room. They were all familiar faces—neighbors, former classmates, even a few elders Tamika had known since she was a child. She felt a surge of relief but also a pang of fear. These were the people she was asking to risk everything, to defy the most powerful force in their community.

Malik greeted her with a firm nod, his face set in determination. "They're all here, Tamika. Every person I spoke to agreed to come."

Tamika glanced around at the small but determined group, her heart swelling with gratitude and resolve. She could see the worry in their eyes, the uncertainty and fear, but also a spark of something else: hope.

Jamal stepped forward, his voice steady as he addressed the group. "I know that being here tonight is a risk. I know that the Circle has kept us all in line with fear, with threats. But we're here because we've all lost something to them. We're here because we're tired of living in fear."

A murmur rippled through the crowd, people nodding in agreement, exchanging looks of encouragement. Tamika felt a surge of pride as she looked at Jamal, seeing the way he commanded the room, the way his words reached the hearts of those gathered.

"We're ready to fight back," Jamal continued, his voice rising with conviction. "But we have to be careful. We have to move in silence, just like they do. We need to be smart, to stay under the radar. Because if the Circle catches us…" He let the words hang in the air, their unspoken threat heavy with meaning.

A silence settled over the room, thick with anticipation. Tamika stepped forward, her heart pounding as she looked at each person in turn. "This is our chance," she said softly, her voice carrying an edge of determination. "If we stay silent, if we let them keep doing what they're doing… then nothing will ever change. But together, we have power. Together, we can break the Circle."

A young woman raised her hand, her expression filled with a mixture of fear and hope. "What exactly are we going to do?" she asked, her voice trembling slightly. "How can we bring down something so big, so… so powerful?"

Tamika took a deep breath, gathering her thoughts. "We start small," she replied. "We gather information, we expose their secrets. The Circle thrives in the shadows, hidden behind lies and fear. If we can bring their actions to light, if we can show people what they really are, then we can weaken their hold on this community."

Another voice spoke up, an older man with a weary look in his eyes. "And if they come after us? If they retaliate?"

Jamal's gaze hardened, his expression resolute. "They will come after us. They will try to silence us. But that's why we're doing this together. Alone, we're vulnerable. But as a group, as a united force, we have a chance."

Tamika watched as the group processed his words, the gravity of their mission settling over them like a weight. She could see the fear in their eyes, the worry and doubt. But she also saw something else—a spark of determination, a sense of purpose that fueled their desire for change.

"We'll move carefully," she continued, her voice steady. "We'll work in small groups, each of us gathering information, keeping each other informed. If anyone notices anything unusual, if anyone suspects they're being watched, we need to act quickly. This isn't just a fight for ourselves; it's a fight for everyone who has been hurt by the Circle, for everyone who deserves a chance to live without fear."

The group nodded, a quiet murmur of agreement filling the room. Tamika felt a rush of hope as she looked around, seeing the strength and resolve in their faces. They were ready. They were tired of living in silence, of letting the Circle control their lives. And now, they had each other.

The meeting continued as they discussed strategies, creating a network of contacts and safe locations, people they could trust and places they could go if things went wrong. Tamika's mind raced with ideas, with plans to expose the Circle's lies, to bring its crimes to light.

But just as they were wrapping up, Malik's phone buzzed with a message. He glanced at the screen, his face going pale as he read the words.

"What is it?" Tamika asked, her heart skipping a beat.

Malik looked up, his eyes wide with fear. "The Circle… they know we're here."

A wave of panic swept through the room, people glancing at each other, their faces filled with alarm. Tamika felt her blood run cold as she realized the gravity of the situation. If the Circle knew about their meeting, then they were all in immediate danger.

"How did they find out?" she asked, her voice trembling.

Malik shook his head, his gaze filled with dread. "I don't know. But we have to leave—now."

The group sprang into action, gathering their belongings and heading for the exits. Tamika's mind raced as she tried to process what was happening. Had they been betrayed? Had someone in their group turned them in? Or was the Circle's network of informants even more extensive than she'd realized?

As they filed out of the warehouse, Tamika felt a surge of fear mingled with anger. She had known the risks, understood the dangers, but the reality of the situation hit her like a punch to the gut. The Circle wasn't just an enemy—they were a force that seemed to anticipate their every move, a shadow that loomed over their lives.

Outside, the group scattered, each person heading in a different direction to avoid drawing attention.

Tamika and Jamal slipped into a nearby alley, keeping to the shadows as they made their way back toward the edge of town. She felt a sense of dread, a creeping fear that someone was watching, that they were being followed.

As they reached a deserted street, Jamal stopped, scanning the darkness. "We need to figure out who tipped them off," he said, his voice filled with frustration. "We can't afford any more slip-ups."

Tamika nodded, her mind racing as she thought about the people they had met with. She wanted to believe they could trust everyone, that they were all united in their mission. But now, doubt gnawed at her, the possibility of betrayal hanging over her like a dark cloud.

"We'll figure it out," she replied, her voice steady despite the fear twisting inside her. "But for now, we need to keep moving. If they're following us…"

She trailed off, her words cut short as she heard the sound of footsteps behind them. Her heart skipped a beat, and she turned, her eyes scanning the darkness.

She saw nothing, but the feeling of being watched, of being hunted, was unmistakable.

"We're not safe here," Jamal whispered, his voice barely audible. "We need to get somewhere they can't follow us."

They took off, moving quickly through the empty streets, their footsteps echoing in the silence. Tamika's mind raced, her thoughts filled with questions, doubts, and a gnawing sense of urgency. The Circle's power was vast, its reach extending into every corner of her life, and she knew that if they didn't find a way to outmaneuver them, they would be caught.

As they reached a hidden back entrance to a local café—a spot they'd used as a temporary hideout before—Tamika felt a surge of relief. She stepped inside, Jamal following close behind, and they locked the door behind them, catching their breath as they settled into the shadows.

For a moment, they sat in silence, the weight of the night pressing down on them. Tamika felt a mixture of fear and anger, a sense of helplessness she hadn't felt in a long time. But as she looked at Jamal, at the determination in his eyes, she knew that they couldn't give up.

"This isn't over," she whispered, her voice filled with resolve. "They may have people everywhere, but so do we. We just have to be smarter, to stay one step ahead."

Jamal nodded, "We'll find a way. They can't keep us down forever."

As they sat in the darkness, planning their next move, Tamika felt a renewed sense of purpose. The Circle was powerful, but they were stronger together. And no matter how many setbacks they faced, she knew that they would continue fighting, continue pushing forward, until they had exposed every last one of the Circle's secrets.

This was just the beginning.

Chapter 11: Unearthing Evidence

The morning light filtered weakly through the café's curtained windows, casting a pale glow across the small room where Tamika and Jamal sat, weary but resolute. The fear from the previous night lingered like a shadow, a reminder that the Circle was always one step behind them, ready to strike at any moment.

But today, they were moving forward with a plan they'd prepared for weeks—a plan to finally gather concrete evidence that could turn the tide of their fight. It was one thing to expose the Circle through rumors and whispers; it was another to reveal hard proof that would force even the most loyal supporters to confront the truth.

"We need to get inside the records room," Jamal said quietly, his voice steady. "That's where they keep everything—documents, finances, even surveillance tapes. If we can access that, we'll have everything we need to expose them."

Tamika nodded, her heart racing at the thought. The records room was located in the back of a well-guarded community center, a building the Circle controlled under the guise of a nonprofit organization. The center was frequently used for community events, but its hidden purpose was to serve as a base for the Circle's operations.

"It won't be easy," she said, glancing at Jamal. "They've got cameras, guards… the place is locked down. If we're caught…"

Jamal shook his head, "We won't get caught. We'll go during a community event—somewhere crowded, somewhere they wouldn't expect us to make a move."

"When's the next event?" she asked, her voice steady despite the dread simmering inside her.

"Tonight," Jamal replied. "A fundraiser. It's open to the whole community—perfect cover for us to blend in."

Tamika took a deep breath, nodding. "Then let's do it."

The community center was bustling that evening, filled with people from every part of town. Tamika and Jamal moved through the crowd with practiced ease, each dressed in casual clothing, blending seamlessly with the guests. The sounds of laughter and conversation filled the air, a thin veneer of normalcy over the building's darker purpose.

As they moved toward the back of the building, Tamika's gaze flicked over the crowd, searching for familiar faces. She spotted several community leaders, people she had once respected—people she now knew were deeply entangled with the Circle's activities. She clenched her fists, forcing herself to stay calm. Tonight wasn't the night to confront them. Tonight, they were here to gather evidence.

Jamal led her down a narrow hallway toward the rear of the building, the sounds of the fundraiser fading into a distant hum. They reached a locked door marked "Staff Only," and Jamal took out a set of lockpicking tools, his hands steady as he worked the lock. Tamika kept watch, her heart pounding as she glanced over her shoulder, half-expecting to see someone coming down the hallway.

After a few tense moments, the lock clicked, and Jamal opened the door, ushering her inside. They stepped into a dark, narrow room lined with file cabinets and shelves stacked with boxes. A small, ancient-looking computer sat on a desk in the corner, its screen dark.

"This is it," Jamal whispered, closing the door quietly behind them.

Tamika nodded, her hands shaking as she moved toward the computer. She knew they didn't have much time; it was only a matter of minutes before someone might notice their absence and start asking questions. She sat down at the desk, powering on the computer and quickly scanning the screen for access points.

Jamal moved to the file cabinets, pulling open drawers and rifling through stacks of papers, his movements quick and efficient. "Look for anything marked 'financials' or 'security,'" he murmured. "Those files will have the details we need."

Tamika's fingers flew across the keyboard, her mind focused as she navigated the computer's files. She opened a folder labeled "Personnel" and began scrolling through the documents, each one filled with names, contact information, and incriminating notes about the people working for the Circle. She recognized some of the names immediately—local officials, community leaders, even a few members of the police force.

"This is it," she whispered, her heart pounding as she saved the files onto a small flash drive she had brought. "This is the proof we need."

But as she continued scanning the files, she stumbled upon a document that made her blood run cold. It was a list of "targeted individuals"—people the Circle had marked as threats. Her heart raced as she scrolled through the names, recognizing friends, neighbors… even Malik.

She felt a surge of panic, her hands shaking as she quickly saved the file. The Circle was watching them more closely than she had realized; they had a list of people they intended to "neutralize," and her allies were among them.

"Jamal," she whispered urgently, glancing over at him. "They know about Malik. They're going after him and others who've spoken out."

Jamal's face tightened, and he closed the file drawer, his expression grim. "Then we have to move fast. The longer we stay, the more danger they're in."

Just as he spoke, the sound of footsteps echoed down the hallway outside. Tamika's heart leapt, and she froze, her mind racing as the footsteps grew louder, coming closer. She looked at Jamal, her eyes wide with fear.

"Hide," he mouthed, motioning for her to get behind one of the file cabinets. She crouched down, her heart pounding in her chest as the footsteps stopped outside the door. She held her breath, listening as the door handle rattled, and then, slowly, the door creaked open.

A flashlight beam swept across the room, illuminating the shelves and file cabinets. Tamika pressed herself further into the shadows, her mind racing as she tried to remain perfectly still. She felt Jamal's hand on her shoulder, steadying her, a silent reassurance that they were in this together.

After a few tense moments, the light flicked off, and the door closed, the footsteps retreating down the hallway. Tamika let out a shaky breath, her body trembling as the adrenaline coursed through her veins.

"We need to go," Jamal whispered, his voice filled with urgency. "Now."

They moved quickly, slipping out of the records room and down the hallway, blending back into the crowd as if nothing had happened. Tamika felt her heart racing, her mind still reeling from the documents she had seen. The Circle wasn't just an organization—it was a network of control, a force that had infiltrated every aspect of their lives. And now, she had proof.

As they left the community center, the cool night air washed over her, clearing her mind and filling her with a renewed sense of purpose. She clutched the flash drive in her pocket, feeling the weight of its contents, the secrets it held.

"We did it," she said softly, glancing at Jamal. "We have the evidence."

Jamal nodded, a faint smile crossing his face. "This is just the beginning, Tamika. With this, we can start to turn people against the Circle. We can show them the truth."

But as they walked, a dark realization crept over her. She had seen the list of targeted individuals, people the Circle intended to "silence." She knew that every day they waited put those people at risk, that every moment they delayed was a chance for the Circle to retaliate.

"We have to move quickly," she said, her voice filled with urgency. "They're going after Malik and the others. If we don't act soon…"

Jamal's expression hardened, and he nodded. "Then we don't wait. We go public. We spread this information far and wide, make sure everyone in this community knows what the Circle is doing."

Tamika took a deep breath, her heart racing with a mixture of fear and excitement. This was the moment they had been waiting for, the chance to finally expose the Circle and bring its secrets into the light. But she knew that once they took this step, there would be no going back.

As they disappeared into the shadows, Tamika felt a surge of determination. The Circle's power was vast, but they now held the key to its downfall. And she was ready to do whatever it took to bring it to an end.

The rebellion had begun.

Chapter 12: The Whispering Walls

The next morning, Tamika awoke with a feeling of purpose she hadn't felt in a long time. She held the flash drive containing the Circle's secrets in her hand, its contents a silent promise that things were about to change. Today, she and Jamal were going public. They planned to release the rest of the documents online, send copies to trusted journalists, and spread word throughout the community more than before.

As she dressed, her phone vibrated with a message. It was from Malik, confirming the location where they'd planned to meet that morning. She felt a sense of relief, grateful for the network of allies who were taking risks alongside her. She knew the stakes, knew that every step closer to exposing the Circle brought them deeper into danger. But it was a danger she was prepared to face.

Tamika grabbed her jacket and headed out; the flash drive tucked safely in her pocket. She and Jamal had agreed to meet in a quiet spot near the edge of town—a secluded, half-finished construction site where no one would think to look for them. She moved through the streets, her eyes scanning every face, every shadow, feeling the weight of the secrets she carried.

When she arrived, Jamal was already waiting, his face tense, he looked nervously around. He gave her a quick nod as she approached, his eyes flicking to the flash drive in her hand.

"Are we ready?" he asked, his voice low and steady.

Tamika nodded, her heart pounding. "Ready as we'll ever be. Once this is out there, the Circle won't be able to hide anymore."

But as they exchanged a determined glance, a faint sound made Tamika's stomach drop—a shuffling from behind one of the nearby walls. She and Jamal exchanged a look, each instantly on guard.

Before they could react, Malik stepped into view, his face pale and his expression one of deep regret. Behind him stood three men, each wearing dark clothing, their faces hardened and their stances intimidating. Tamika recognized them instantly; they were members of the Circle.

"Malik?" she whispered, her voice a mix of disbelief and betrayal. "What... what is this?"

Malik's eyes darted between her and Jamal, his hands trembling. "I'm sorry, Tamika. I didn't have a choice. They... they found out about our plans. They threatened my family. I had to tell them."

Tamika felt a wave of cold wash over her, her mind racing. She had trusted Malik, believed in him, and now he was standing there with members of the very organization they had been working to expose. The realization hit her like a punch to the gut. Their plans were compromised, their rebellion betrayed before it had even begun.

One of the men stepped forward, his eyes fixed on Tamika. "You've been very busy, haven't you?" he sneered, his voice dripping with menace. "Gathering information, spreading lies about the Circle. You really thought you could get away with it?"

Tamika felt her fists clench, her anger boiling over. "They aren't lies. Everything on this flash drive proves what you've done. The people in this community deserve to know the truth."

The man smirked, his gaze cold. "The truth? The truth is whatever we decide it is, and you're about to learn that the hard way."

He reached forward, his hand outstretched toward her pocket. She felt Jamal tense beside her, his body shifting, ready to defend her. But she knew that fighting now would be futile; they were outnumbered and cornered. Reluctantly, she handed over the flash drive, her heart sinking as the man pocketed it with a satisfied smile.

"Thank you," he said mockingly. "This little crusade of yours ends here."

Tamika's mind raced, desperation clawing at her as she watched her months of hard work slip away in an instant. But as she glanced at Jamal, she saw a flicker of determination in his eyes—a silent message that their fight wasn't over.

"Maybe you can take the evidence," Jamal said, his voice steady, "but you can't silence everyone. People already know about the Circle. They're ready to fight back."

The man's smile faded, replaced by a cold glare. "We'll see about that," he replied, his voice low and menacing. He turned to Malik, his expression darkening. "Make sure they don't cause any more trouble."

Malik nodded reluctantly, his gaze filled with guilt and sorrow as he looked at Tamika and Jamal. She could see the regret in his eyes, the pain of a man forced to choose between his friends and his family. But that didn't lessen the sting of betrayal, the feeling of being abandoned by someone she had trusted.

As the men led her and Jamal away from the construction site, Tamika's mind raced with thoughts of escape, plans to turn the tables on the Circle. She knew they were being taken somewhere to be "dealt with," and the thought sent a shiver down her spine. But she refused to give up, refused to let them win.

They were led into a waiting car, where two of the men sat on either side of them, their expressions cold and unyielding. Tamika's heart pounded as the car started moving, carrying them away from the town, from the people they had fought to protect.

After what felt like an eternity, the car pulled up to a secluded clearing on the outskirts of the city. The men got out, dragging Tamika and Jamal with them. She stumbled as they pulled her from the car, her mind racing with fear and desperation.

One of the men shoved her roughly, his gaze filled with contempt. "You thought you could expose us?" he sneered. "You're nothing. Just another mouth to shut."

Jamal shot the man a glare, his face filled with defiance. "You think silencing us will stop people from finding out what you've done? The truth will come out, no matter what you do."

The man's expression hardened, and he stepped toward Jamal, his hand clenched into a fist. But before he could strike, the sound of sirens pierced the air, cutting through the tension like a blade. The men froze, their heads snapping toward the road as the flashing lights of police cars appeared in the distance.

Tamika felt a surge of hope, her heart pounding as she realized that someone must have called for help. She didn't know who, didn't know how they'd been found, but at that moment, it didn't matter. The Circle's control was slipping, and she was determined to seize the chance.

The men exchanged glances, their expressions filled with frustration and anger. One of them cursed under his breath, motioning for the others to get back in the car. They left without another word, their departure abrupt and filled with a sense of unfinished business. As the police cars pulled up, Tamika felt a wave of relief wash over her.

She turned to Jamal, her face filled with a mixture of exhaustion and hope. "We're not done yet," she said, her voice steady despite the fear that lingered in her chest.

Jamal nodded, his gaze filled with determination. "No. This is just the beginning."

As they spoke with the police, giving statements and explaining their ordeal, Tamika felt a renewed sense of purpose. The Circle had tried to silence them, tried to crush their rebellion before it could begin, but they had failed. The truth was still within reach, and she knew that their fight was far from over.

They left the scene that night with a plan, a quiet determination that burned brighter than ever. The Circle's grip was loosening, and Tamika was ready to see their power unravel, one secret at a time.

This was only the beginning.

Chapter 13: The Silent Alliance

The morning after their harrowing escape, Tamika sat in a dim, quiet café, nursing a cup of bitter coffee as she waited for Jamal to arrive. The events of the previous night still haunted her—the betrayal, the fear, the feeling of being completely outmatched by an enemy that seemed omnipresent. She stared into her coffee, wondering if they'd ever truly be able to bring the Circle to its knees.

But as the café door opened and Jamal stepped in, her thoughts solidified into a fierce resolve. The Circle had tried to silence them, but they had survived. And if she had learned anything from the past few days, it was that their survival meant they were a genuine threat.

Jamal slid into the seat across from her, his face etched with fatigue and determination. "I've been thinking," he began without preamble. "If we're going to go after the Circle, we can't do it alone. We need more people, people with real power."

Tamika nodded, already seeing the plan forming in her mind. "Agreed. We've been moving in the shadows, trying to expose them quietly, but that's not enough anymore. If we want to really make an impact, we need a coalition. We need people who are just as committed as we are."

Jamal leaned forward, his gaze intense. "There's a group I know of—defectors from the Circle, people who got out years ago. They call themselves the Silent Alliance. They've been operating quietly, under the radar, gathering information, finding ways to protect people the Circle has targeted. If we could find them… they might be willing to help."

Tamika felt a flicker of hope at his words. She had heard rumors of such a group, whispers of people who had managed to escape the Circle's grasp and were now working from the shadows to undermine its power. But she had never believed they were real—until now.

"Do you know where to find them?" she asked, her voice filled with cautious optimism.

Jamal nodded. "I have a contact—a woman named Leah. She used to be high up in the Circle's ranks, but she left years ago. She's been helping people go underground, finding them safe places when the Circle comes after them. If anyone can put us in touch with the Alliance, it's her."

Tamika's heart raced as she listened, feeling a renewed sense of hope. The Silent Alliance represented everything she had been fighting for—a force of people who, like her, had seen the darkness of the Circle and refused to accept it. She knew that with their help, they would stand a real chance against the Circle's power.

"Then let's find her," she said, her voice steady. "The sooner we reach out, the better. The Circle already know we're a threat. We can't waste any time."

Jamal nodded, a glimmer of determination in his eyes. "I'll set up a meeting. But we have to be careful. Leah has spent years hiding from the Circle. She's not going to take kindly to anyone who seems like they might be a risk."

Tamika's mind raced with possibilities, her determination building as they discussed their next steps. She knew that meeting with the Alliance was risky, but it was a risk worth taking. If they could form an alliance with people who shared their goal, people who understood the danger of going up against the Circle, they would be stronger than ever.

That evening, Jamal took her to an unmarked building on the outskirts of town. It was a plain, nondescript structure, the kind of place people passed without a second glance. But as they stepped inside, Tamika felt a tension in the air, a sense of anticipation that made her pulse quicken.

Leah was already there, waiting in the dimly lit room. She was a tall woman with sharp eyes and a quiet strength that radiated from her every movement. She didn't smile as they approached, but Tamika could see a glimmer of curiosity in her gaze.

"So, you're the ones stirring up trouble," Leah said, her voice low and guarded. "Jamal speaks highly of you, Tamika. Says you're committed, that you've got the kind of resolve we need."

Tamika met Leah's gaze, her heart pounding as she replied, "The Circle has controlled this community for too long. They've hurt too many people, destroyed too many lives. We want to expose them, to bring their crimes to light. But we need help. We can't do it alone."

Leah studied her for a long moment, her expression unreadable. "The Silent Alliance isn't a group you can just join," she said finally. "It's not an organization, not in the traditional sense. It's a network—a network of people who understand what it means to live in the shadows, to fight without ever being seen."

"We're not asking to join," Jamal interjected. "We're asking for an alliance. We want to bring down the Circle, and we know that together, we'll be stronger."

Leah considered his words. After a moment, she nodded, a faint smile tugging at the corner of her mouth. "You've got guts, I'll give you that. But understand this—if you join forces with us, there's no turning back. Once you're in, you're in for life. And if you betray us…" Her voice trailed off, her meaning clear.

Tamika felt a surge of respect for Leah's caution. She knew that the Alliance couldn't afford to trust easily, that betrayal was a constant threat in their world. But she also knew that this was their best chance to fight back, to gather the strength they needed to bring down the Circle.

"We understand," she said quietly. "We're in this for the long haul."

Leah nodded, a look of approval in her eyes. "Then welcome to the fight. We'll need to move carefully, but with the Alliance's resources, we can start making real progress. We've been gathering evidence on the Circle for years—names, dates, transactions. And we've been working to protect people, to give them a way out."

A spark of hope ignited in Tamika's chest. With the Alliance's help, they would have the resources, the information, and the allies they needed to turn the tide. She could already see the pieces falling into place, their quiet rebellion gaining momentum.

But Leah's expression turned serious. "There's one more thing you need to know. The Circle has informants everywhere. They've got people on the inside, people who pretend to be allies but are loyal to the Circle. You can't trust anyone fully—not even your closest friends."

Tamika's heart sank at the warning, the reality of their situation settling over her like a heavy weight. She had already seen betrayal up close, felt the sting of it in Malik's actions. But hearing Leah's words brought the danger into sharp focus. They were walking a tightrope, and one wrong move could cost them everything.

"We'll be careful," she replied, her voice filled with resolve. "We've come this far. We're not giving up now."

Leah nodded, "Good. Then let's get to work."

In the days that followed, Tamika and Jamal worked tirelessly with the Alliance, meeting in secret, exchanging information, and building a network of allies who were just as committed to exposing the Circle. They moved in the shadows, careful to avoid detection, knowing that the Circle's informants could be anywhere.

For the first time, Tamika felt a glimmer of hope—a sense that, despite the risks, they were making progress. The Alliance's resources were vast, their knowledge of the Circle's operations extensive. And with every piece of information they uncovered, every name they added to their list, Tamika felt a step closer to their ultimate goal.

But even as they moved forward, the danger loomed ever closer. They knew that the Circle was watching, waiting for the slightest misstep. And as the Alliance's plans grew bolder, the stakes became higher, the risks more daunting.

Tamika steeled herself, her resolve unshaken. She knew that the road ahead would be treacherous, filled with threats and uncertainty. But she was ready, her heart filled with a fierce determination that burned brighter with every passing day.

This was a battle she was willing to fight, a fight for freedom, for justice, for everyone the Circle had silenced. And she knew, with a certainty that strengthened her resolve, that no matter how dark the path became, she would see it through to the end.

The rebellion was no longer just a hope, it was a reality. And she was ready to face whatever came next.

Chapter 14: Echoes of Betrayal

It was late evening, and the dim, flickering lights in the underground meeting room cast shadows that danced across the walls. The tension in the room was palpable. Tamika could feel the weight of the upcoming mission pressing down on her, filling the silence between her and the other members of the Alliance who had gathered here tonight. They were close—closer than ever—to exposing the Circle's innermost secrets.

Leah had called this emergency meeting after receiving information from one of her own informants within the Circle's inner circle, a man they only knew as "M." His intelligence had been invaluable, leading them to crucial documents and locations that revealed the Circle's influence over the police, schools, and even local businesses. But tonight, "M" had given them something else—something that could potentially destroy the Circle entirely.

"We're hitting the heart of the Circle's operations," Leah said, her voice steady and commanding. "Tonight, we're going after the vault."

The word "vault" hung in the air, a powerful symbol of the Circle's most protected assets. According to "M," the vault contained records, financial documents, and video evidence of the Circle's most heinous crimes, hidden deep within a fortified basement in one of the city's oldest buildings. It was the kind of evidence that, if exposed, would dismantle the Circle and implicate every high-ranking member in their crimes.

Leah turned to Tamika and Jamal, her gaze sharp. "We need people who can move quietly, who understand the risks. If we're caught, this doesn't just end for us—it ends for everyone we're trying to protect."

Tamika nodded, feeling her pulse quicken. She had come this far, had sacrificed too much to turn back now. The idea of finally striking at the Circle's heart, of holding in her hands the proof that could set her community free, was too powerful to resist.

"I'm in," she said, her voice steady. "Tell us what we need to do."

Jamal nodded in agreement, his gaze filled with determination. Leah outlined the plan: they would enter the building posing as workers for a late-night maintenance shift. Once inside, they would need to evade the security guards, access the basement vault, and download the files onto a secure drive. It was a risky plan, but if they pulled it off, it would be the Circle's downfall.

As Leah finished explaining, she paused, her gaze scanning the room. "There's one more thing," she said, her voice laced with caution. "M has warned us that there's a traitor in our ranks—someone feeding information back to the Circle."

A murmur rippled through the room, each member exchanging wary glances. Tamika felt her heart skip a beat, a wave of dread washing over her. The last time they had faced betrayal, Malik had led them straight into the Circle's hands. She didn't want to believe it could happen again, but Leah's words left no room for doubt.

"We don't know who it is yet," Leah continued, "but we have to assume they're watching every move we make. Keep your guard up, and trust no one entirely."

The weight of Leah's words settled over Tamika like a shroud, her mind racing as she considered the possibility that someone close to them was working against them. The thought made her stomach twist, but she pushed it aside, focusing on the mission. They couldn't afford to let fear slow them down.

Leah finished the meeting with a final nod of encouragement. "This is our chance. If we get that evidence, we'll bring the Circle to its knees. Stay sharp, stay together, and we'll see this through."

The building that housed the vault was quiet and unassuming, its old stone exterior blending seamlessly with the surrounding architecture. Tamika and Jamal entered through a side door, dressed in maintenance uniforms, their IDs forged by members of the Alliance. They moved quickly, following Leah's instructions, each step bringing them closer to the vault and the secrets it held.

As they descended a narrow staircase toward the basement, Tamika felt her nerves begin to fray. Every sound seemed amplified in the silence, every shadow a potential threat. But Jamal's steady presence beside her kept her focused, reminding her of the purpose that had brought her here.

They reached the basement door, and Jamal quickly went to work on the lock, his movements precise and controlled. Within moments, the door clicked open, revealing a narrow corridor lined with reinforced doors. At the end of the hallway was the vault—an imposing metal door that seemed to pulse with the weight of the secrets it contained.

"This is it," Jamal whispered, his voice barely audible. "Once we open this door, there's no going back."

Tamika nodded, her gaze fixed on the vault. "Then let's finish this."

Jamal entered the code Leah had provided, and the lock clicked open. They stepped into the vault, their eyes adjusting to the dim light that illuminated rows of filing cabinets, shelves lined with binders, and a large metal cabinet that seemed to hold the most sensitive information. Tamika's heart raced as she moved to the cabinet, pulling out the hard drive they'd brought.

They worked quickly, downloading files and photographing documents that exposed the Circle's network of informants, its financial backers, and the list of people it had silenced over the years. Each file was a testament to the Circle's cruelty, a reminder of the lives it had destroyed in its quest for power.

But just as Tamika was finishing, a sound outside the vault made her freeze—a faint but unmistakable shuffle of footsteps. She exchanged a panicked look with Jamal, her mind racing as the footsteps grew louder, closer.

"Someone's coming," she whispered, her voice filled with dread.

Jamal moved toward the door, peeking through the narrow gap. His face paled, and he turned back to her, his expression filled with urgency. "It's Leah," he whispered. "And… someone else."

Tamika's heart sank as she heard voices outside, low and urgent. She recognized Leah's voice, calm and steady, but the other voice sent a chill through her. It was familiar, laced with a cruel edge that she had hoped never to hear again.

It was Malik.

She felt a surge of anger and betrayal, her mind reeling. Malik hadn't just betrayed them once; he had been working with the Circle the entire time, playing them, feeding them information while pretending to help. And now he was here, with Leah, the one person they thought they could trust.

The voices grew louder, and Tamika pressed herself against the wall, her mind racing as she considered their options. She knew they couldn't confront them directly—not without risking everything they had worked for. But as she looked at Jamal, she saw a flash of defiance in his eyes.

"We can't leave without this evidence," he whispered, his voice filled with determination. "We have to find a way out."

Tamika nodded, her mind racing as she scanned the room, searching for an escape route. She settled on a small, grated ventilation shaft near the back of the room. It was narrow, but if they moved quickly, they might be able to squeeze through before Leah and Malik realized they were inside.

Without a word, they moved to the shaft, prying it open as quietly as possible. Tamika climbed in first, the metal walls pressing against her as she crawled forward, each movement slow and careful. Jamal followed, the soft sound of his breathing filling the confined space as they moved through the darkness.

They crawled in silence, each of them hyper-aware of the danger that lurked just beyond the walls. The shaft opened into a dark, empty room on the far side of the building, and Tamika climbed out, her heart pounding as she helped Jamal through.

They took a moment to catch their breath, the weight of their narrow escape settling over them. Tamika felt a surge of relief, but it was quickly overshadowed by anger—anger at Malik, at Leah, at the Circle and everything it represented.

"We have to warn the others," she whispered, her voice filled with urgency. "Leah's working with the Circle. She's been feeding them information this whole time."

Jamal nodded, his gaze filled with determination. "We'll get this evidence out. And we'll expose Leah for what she is."

As they slipped into the night, Tamika felt a renewed sense of purpose. The betrayal had cut deep, but it had also given her clarity. She knew now that their fight wasn't just against the Circle—it was against everyone who upheld its power, everyone who had betrayed their own community for personal gain.

The road ahead would be dangerous, filled with uncertainty and risk. But as she clutched the drive filled with the Circle's secrets, she knew that this was a fight worth waging.

The Circle's days were numbered, and she was ready to see it fall.

Chapter 15: The Price of Freedom

The night air was cold, biting against Tamika's skin as she stood alone on the quiet rooftop, the city's lights stretching out before her. The events of the past few days replayed in her mind: Leah's betrayal, Malik's deception, the daring escape with the evidence, and the moment they finally uploaded it all. The Circle's secrets were no longer hidden, their crimes now laid bare for the world to see. She should have felt relief, maybe even victory, but instead, a dark unease gnawed at her.

Jamal approached from behind, his footsteps soft, his face drawn with exhaustion. He joined her at the edge of the rooftop, staring out at the city that had both shaped them and scarred them.

"It's done," he said quietly, his voice filled with a mix of triumph and caution. "Sandra published everything. The Circle's reach, their crimes, it's all out there. They can't hide anymore."

Tamika nodded, her gaze distant. "It feels... surreal. Like this battle is over, but another one is just beginning."

Jamal's expression darkened. "The Circle won't go down without a fight. They still have people—people in power who will do anything to keep their secrets buried."

As they spoke, Tamika's phone buzzed with a notification. She glanced at the screen, her heart pounding as she read the message: "You think you know the Circle's secrets. But you've only scratched the surface. This isn't over."

Her stomach twisted with dread. She showed the message to Jamal, who took a step back, his face filled with disbelief and anger.

"They're still watching us," he muttered, clenching his fists. "They know everything we've done, even now."

Another message came through, this time with a video attachment. Tamika opened it, her blood running cold as the video began to play. It showed a dark room, barely lit, with a figure seated in a chair, bound and gagged. She recognized the person instantly—it was Malik.

The video's grainy footage captured the unmistakable fear in his eyes, his silent pleas for help. But as Tamika's horror deepened, another figure stepped into the frame, shrouded in shadows, only their outline visible. The figure held up a note to the camera, a single message scrawled in bold, dark letters:

"We're everywhere."

Tamika's hand trembled as she gripped the phone, her mind racing. Malik wasn't just a pawn; he was leverage, a warning. The Circle wasn't defeated—they were regrouping, lurking in the shadows, more dangerous than ever.

"We need to get him out," Tamika whispered, her voice filled with determination.

Jamal nodded, but his face betrayed a flicker of doubt. "They're baiting us, Tamika. This isn't just about Malik. They're showing us that we're not safe—that they'll come after everyone we care about."

Another message appeared on her screen, this one with an address. Her heart pounded as she recognized it: it was an old, abandoned warehouse on the outskirts of the city—the place where the Circle first tried to recruit her, the same place where this battle had truly begun.

Tamika looked at Jamal, her voice trembling with a mixture of fear and resolve. "They want us to go there. It's a trap, but we don't have a choice. If we want to end this, we have to face them."

Jamal's gaze hardened. "Then we go together. But we need backup—anyone from the Alliance who's still loyal, anyone willing to fight."

The two of them shared a final, silent moment of understanding. They had reached the thin line between freedom and fear, and they knew that crossing it meant leaving safety behind. The Circle was everywhere, its reach extending far beyond what they had imagined.

As they descended the rooftop stairs, Tamika's phone buzzed once more. She looked down, her breath catching as she read the words:

"If you come, come alone. This is your last warning."

She looked at Jamal, her voice steady. "We don't have a choice. We go in, and we finish this."

But deep down, she knew that finishing it might cost them everything. As they stepped out into the night, Tamika felt the weight of her decision, the knowledge that she was facing an enemy that wouldn't hesitate to destroy everyone she loved.

And as they disappeared into the shadows, heading toward the place where it all began, a single thought echoed in her mind:

This isn't the end. It's only the beginning.